To:

From:

How to catch a Witch

From the New York Times Bestselling Series

Alice Walstead & Megan Joyce

Based on designs by Andy Elkerton

sourcebooks
wonderland

We happily dressed in our costumes with care,
getting ready for trick-or-treat night.
What we yet didn't know was who else had a plan
for **HALLOWEEN** mischief to give us a fright!

The pumpkins were carved and lit from within
as we walked in the crisp autumn air.
We started to notice ghosts, ghouls, and goblins
popping up over here, there, and **everywhere**!

But there aren't enough kids living in our town
to account for this many CREATURES...
Some of these beings just might be real!
Take a look at all their weird features.

Time to Floss, Bump, and

Up very high was a witch in the sky.
On her broom, she had invites to carry.
With a wave of her wand, the music began.
When dancing, the ghosts looked less scary!

We figured out that the witch brought the creatures,
so we set traps for a Halloween **prize**.
We have to catch her to send all the ghouls back!
It won't be easy 'cause this witch is wise.

BRISTLES

Beyond catching the witch, there's candy to get—
chocolates and sweets big and small.
If the tricks, treats, and traps all fall in line,
this spooky night, we might have it all.

WHOOOSH!

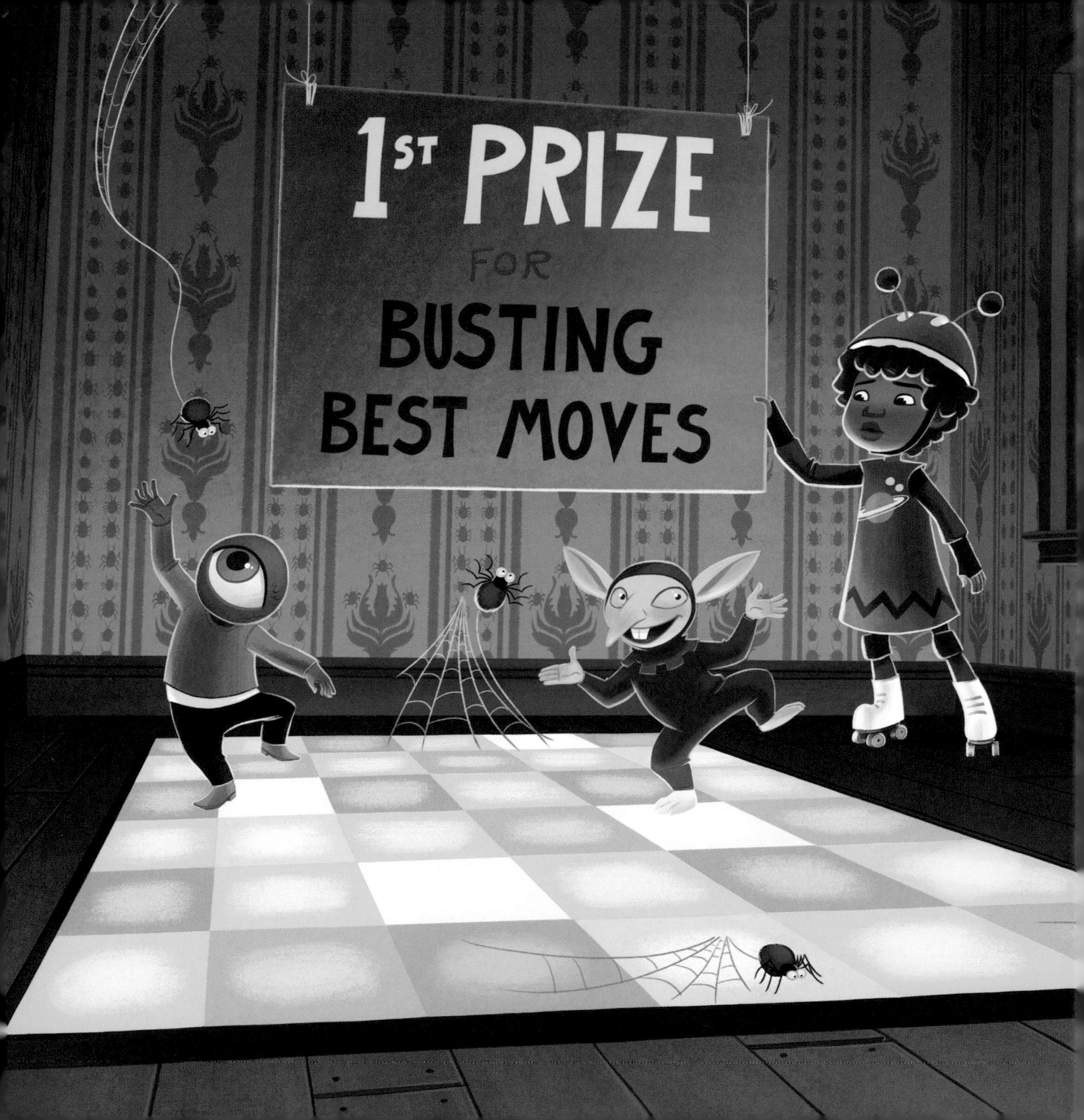
1ST PRIZE
FOR
BUSTING
BEST MOVES

She likes spiders and maybe their webs can help out.
The witch could get stuck on the floor.
Hang on a second... Wait just a minute!
Do we have more kids than **before**?

This witch is clever,
and brought lots of friends.
We need far better traps
before this night ends!

Zombies, dinos, ghosts, wolves, and more!
Monsters everywhere and one in a pool.
We can't catch them all in just one night.
Better trap the witch before ghouls RULE my school!

This is getting serious. We're running out of time.
Do witches even stop for roadblocks?
Sure hope she falls for a **Tunnel of Tricks**.
We need to return our dad's toolbox!

The witch stops her **boogie** to come and explore,
wondering what tricks are inside.
She's wise to the trap and summons some help,
sending a bat in first as her guide.

ENTER
HERE

We watched the boat to see when to start.
She skipped the boat and just used her broom.
Makes sense, we guess, why wouldn't she fly?
We had no idea that thing had such *zoom*!

The dance party had hit the finale at last,
each dancing monster started to cheer!
There's no doubt about it, we have to admit:
This witch threw the party of the year!

Then, just when we thought it was over
and all the goblins were with us forever,
the witch opened a **portal**, and they left in a flash.
As party hostess, she's welcome whenever!

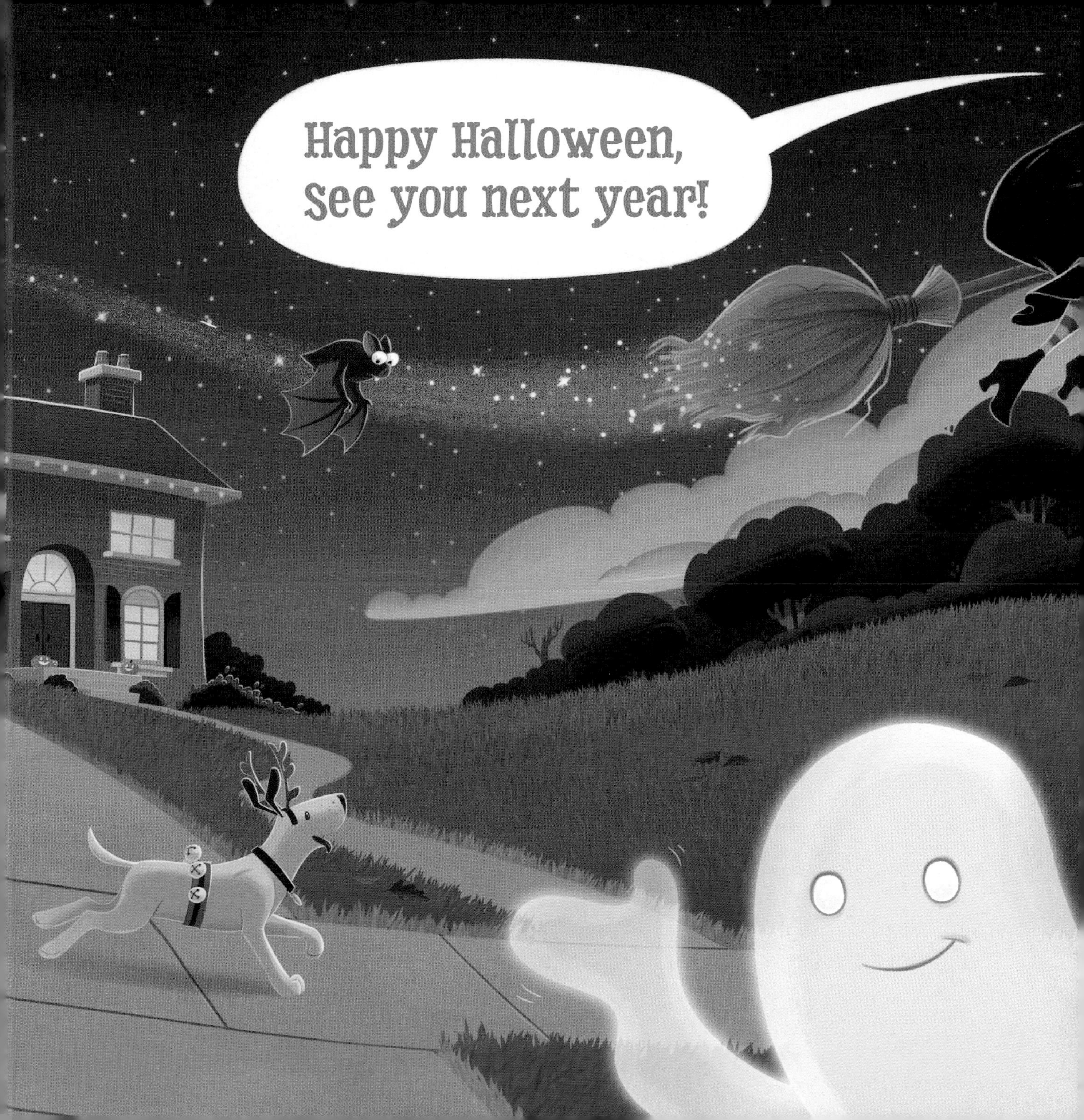
Happy Halloween,
See you next year!

Copyright © 2022 by Sourcebooks
Text by Alice Walstead
Illustrations by Megan Joyce, based on designs by Andy Elkerton
Cover and internal design © 2022 by Sourcebooks

Sourcebooks and the colophon are registered trademarks of Sourcebooks.

All rights reserved. The characters and events portrayed in this book are fictitious or are used fictitiously. Any similarity to real persons, living or dead, is purely coincidental and not intended by the author.

All brand names and product names used in this book are trademarks, registered trademarks, or trade names of their respective holders. Sourcebooks is not associated with any product or vendor in this book.

The art was first sketched, then painted digitally in Photoshop with a Wacom Cintiq tablet.

Published by Sourcebooks Wonderland, an imprint of Sourcebooks Kids
P.O. Box 4410, Naperville, Illinois 60567-4410
(630) 961-3900
sourcebookskids.com

Cataloging-in-Publication Data is on file with the Library of Congress.

Source of Production: Worzalla, Stevens Point, Wisconsin, USA
Date of Production: June 2022
Run Number: 5024571

Printed and bound in the United States of America.

WOZ 10 9 8 7 6 5 4 3 2